THE ADVEN... OF DAVID

BY G.D. HOWE

THUNDERBOLT
BIKE

◆ FriesenPress

Suite 300 - 990 Fort St
Victoria, BC, V8V 3K2
Canada

www.friesenpress.com

ISBN
978-1-5255-7465-8 (Hardcover)
978-1-5255-7466-5 (Paperback)
978-1-5255-7467-2 (eBook)

1. JUVENILE FICTION, ACTION & ADVENTURE

Distributed to the trade by The Ingram Book Company

THANK YOU...

Thank you to my wife and son for their support and love on this adventure. I love you both. Thanks to my family for the support and help through school with my dyslexia. I hope this book is an inspiration to other children with learning disabilities.

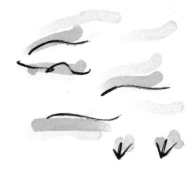

David had been saving his allowance for weeks to order a Thunderbolt Bike. It was the fastest one around; it even had a speed odometer on it. He went to bed dreaming about the bike being delivered tomorrow morning and was very excited about it!

Have you ever been **that excited** about something?

When the bike arrived, David was so excited. He decided to go for a new adventure in the Willow Forest. No kid had ever gone into it before because it was very spooky. He was riding his Thunderbolt bike so fast! He felt like a thunderstorm rolling through the forest as he passed by the old willow trees. He was so amazed at how fast the bike was going that he looked down at the speed odometer to check the speed. He didn't notice the branch in front of him. And it had a big python snake on it.

We all know what happens when you don't pay attention!

David smashed into the tree branch and was thrown from his bike. The snake flew into the sky like a shot from a gun! David had never seen a snake fly before. It was a sight to see! He didn't think anybody would believe him.

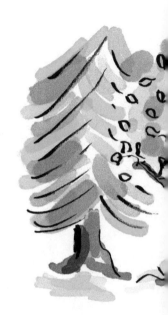

Can you image

what the snake's face

looked like?

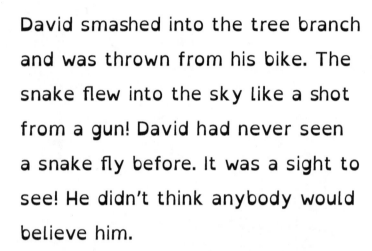

David checked to see if he was hurt. He got up and
went to get his bike. David heard a noise, and
he stopped, scared, as the noise came near.
The noise was heavy breathing, growling, and
a scary laugh. David knew there was trouble
brewing. He looked around and saw....red eyes
watching him! The eyes glowed bright red
like a stop light. David jumped on his bike
and started riding. He was glad his bike was so
fast! He heard heavy breathing, and branches
snapping like they were breaking in a storm!

What do you think it was?

David was really scared. He turned around and saw a creature staring at him. It jumped out of the bushes.

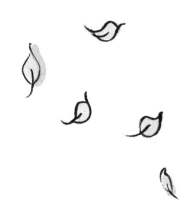

It was a nasty troll!

It had eight eyes and a horn in the middle of its head. It's fur was black, and it had two big feet and six arms—three on each side. It was huge, ten feet tall at least, and weighed a lot. And it had razor sharp teeth!

The troll chased after him. David jumped off his bike and it rolled into some thorny, prickly pine bushes. David ran and ran to look for a place to hide. He heard the troll behind him! It kept roaring! He found a cave and struggled to crawl into it. David hoped the troll couldn't reach him inside the cave.

David moved as close to the far wall as he could. The troll was growling and tearing at the cave entrance. It stuck one of its mean, hairy, gross hands into the cave to reach David, but couldn't fit the rest of its arm in. It was roaring the whole time. David's ears hurt as the troll screamed loudly to get to him.

What should David do next?

As David crawled away from the cave entrance,
the troll stuck its ugly face and its eight eyes
into the cave entrance. Then, the troll started
hitting the cave—it sure was mad! David
thought the ceiling might fall down on him.
He jumped back near the cave wall. Then,
David's hand slipped into a hole.

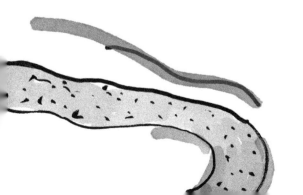

David found a little tunnel that went underground. He noticed it led out somewhere. He crawled through the tunnel and it came to an end at a leafy bush. David moved the brush aside and reached his hand straight up out of the hole. He felt fur; looking up, he saw the troll. Luckily, the troll was so mad that it didn't feel David touching its fur. David crawled out as quiet as a mouse and scampered to the trees.

David looked back to see if the troll had seen him. It hadn't! He kept walking and then,

"Snap!"

a twig broke. The troll turned and looked with a mean face. The troll ran after him, and David began to run. The troll ran slowly because it didn't want to get anything in its eyes.

Somebody grabbed David from behind and pulled him behind a willow tree. Then, the person put a hand over his mouth and said, "Shhhh, be quiet." David turned around and saw a young homeless man. The troll got mad and started tearing trees and bushes up, until hardly anything was left. The homeless man and David kept crawling as quiet as field mice.

Finally, they got behind some rocks and started running. The troll didn't hear them. As they got to the hut that was on the other side of the forest, the man and David went inside. The homeless man said, "My name is Buddy. What's your name young man?" David told him his name. Buddy asked, "How did you get here?" David said. "Oh, I just—" Then he remembered. "My bike, my new bike! I begged Mom for it, and spent all my savings. My Thunderbolt bike! I've got to go back for it!"

Buddy said, "You looking for this?" And he pulled out... the Thunderbolt Bike! David asked, "Where did you get that?" Buddy said, "I found it in the thorny brushes as I was walking around looking for berries to eat. It was all muddy, so I cleaned it off. I heard a loud crushing noise and I knew it had to be the mean troll. Every time someone comes in here, they never leave." David said, "Thank you. I thought the troll would break it."

Buddy laughed and said, "No, the troll isn't very smart." David said, "That troll was tearing that cave up like wrapping paper." David was still scared. Then, the hut started to shake.

It was the troll!

Buddy told David to go out the back door and ride as fast as he could to safety. Buddy said, "I'll distract the troll." David burst out the door on his bike like a raging storm, not looking back. He rode his bike straight home.

When he got there, he dropped his bike and ran into the house. David started yelling, "*Mom, Mom!* You won't believe what happened to me! There's a troll in the willow forest and this nice homeless man named Buddy helped save me." David's mom laughed and chuckled. She said, "David, you have such an active imagination. Sweetheart, where did you get the big egg-sized bump on your head from?" David stopped for a minute to think.

Was the troll real?

Was it all just his imagination, or did it really happen?

What do you think?

CPSIA information can be obtained
at www.ICGtesting.com
Printed in the USA
BVHW021708290921
617766BV00009B/252